The Seedling

that didn't want to grow

Britta Teckentrup

PRESTEL

Munich · London · New York

It was spring

and all of the seeds in the ground were ready to grow.

They all grew tall and straight, just as they were supposed to do.

All but one...

One little seed hadn't grown at all.

"I wonder what's wrong?,"

said Ladybird.

"Let's just sit next to her and wait.

Maybe she needs more time?,"

replied Ant.

Ant was right.

Very soon the seed grew small roots

and tiny green leaves started to appear.

Her life was about to begin.

She looked so delicate and fragile –

Ant and Ladybird fell in love with her

immediately.

It was dark on the meadow ground.

By now the other plants had grown so tall and wide that they blocked

out all of the sunshine.

So the little seedling began her journey in search of the sun.

"Let's go with her!," said Ant.

The seedling grew fast, and soon the animals of the meadow
came to join her on her difficult adventure.

Ant and Ladybird were so proud of their brave little friend.

The seedling changed with every day.

Tiny leaves turned into bigger leaves;

she formed deep roots and grew stronger and stronger.

The seedling had become a little plant and was weaving

and winding her way through the undergrowth.

Her friends were always by her side and helped the best they could.

Cricket guarded her roots.

Mouse searched for the easiest paths ahead.

And Butterfly and Ladybird flew high above trying to find the perfect spot for her.

Finally the day arrived when the meadow undergrowth became thinner. For the first time the little plant could feel the warm summer sun on her leaves.

She knew this spot would be the perfect place.

And then everything happened quickly.

The little plant grew taller and taller and branched out.

Buds started to appear, and they soon transformed into
hundreds of blossoms. The little plant wasn't so little anymore...
Her friends watched her transformation in amazement.

Through the long, hot
days of summer she was
the happiest plant
there could be.
All kinds of animals
lived among her
many leaves.
She was full of
love and life.

Many weeks and months passed by,
and the days started to get shorter and colder.
Autumn was around the corner.

The leaves of the plant had turned
as golden as the October sky,
and she was gently swaying
in the autumn breeze.

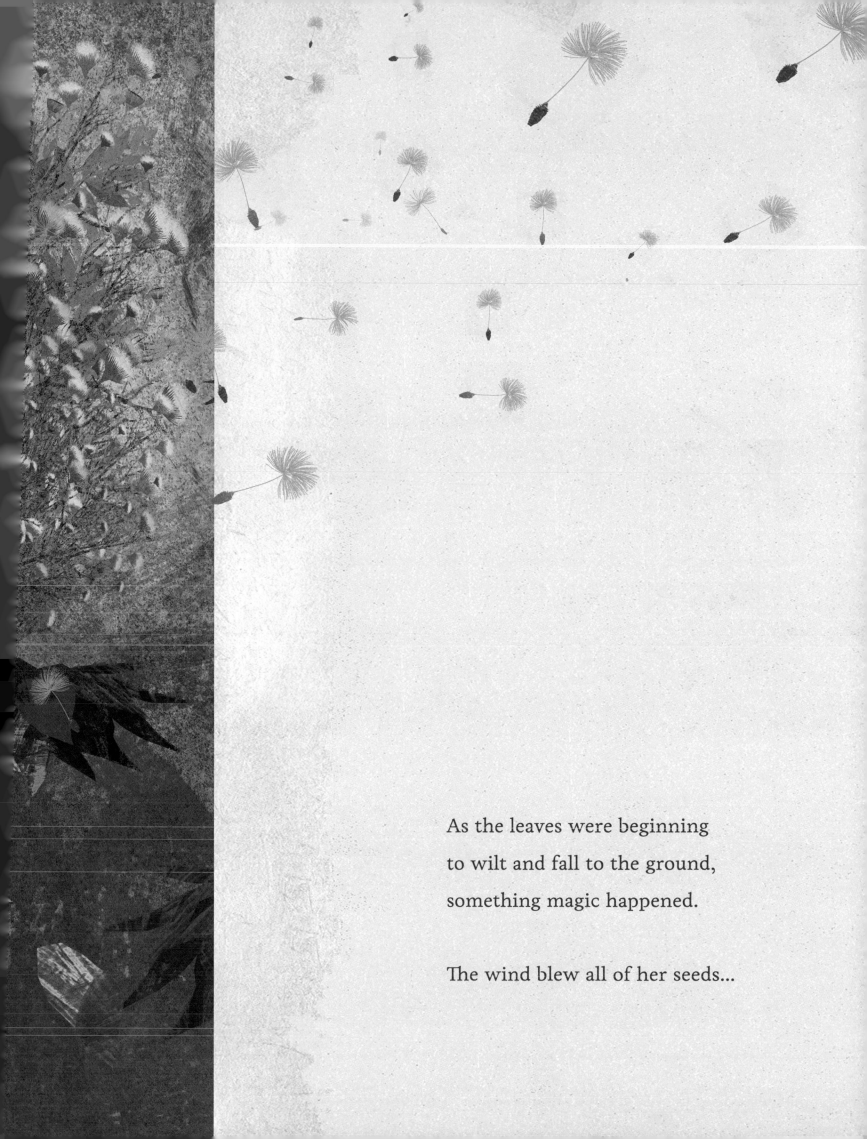

As the leaves were beginning
to wilt and fall to the ground,
something magic happened.

The wind blew all of her seeds...

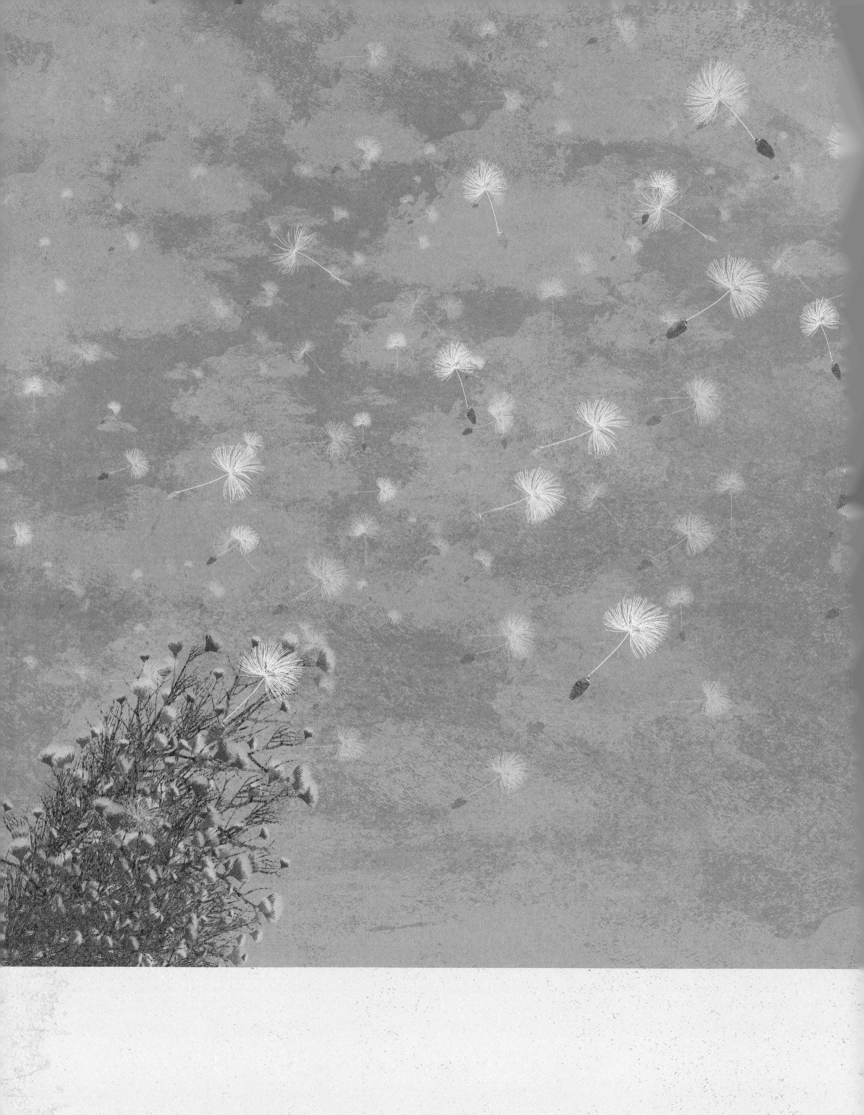

... far and wide.

And then everything turned grey and cold.

It was time for the final goodbye.

Little Mouse made a wish...

"I wish that I will see you again,"

she whispered with a tear in her eye.

Snow covered the meadow like a soft blanket and everything went silent.

Winter seemed to last forever...

Until it was spring again and
all of the new seeds in the ground were ready to grow.

© 2020, 2. Auflage 2021,
Prestel Verlag, Munich · London · New York
A member of Penguin Random House Verlagsgruppe GmbH
Neumarkter Strasse 28 · 81673 Munich
© Illustrations and text: Britta Teckentrup, 2021

Library of Congress Control Number: 2019950495
A CIP catalogue record for this book is available
from the British Library.

Editorial direction: Doris Kutschbach
Project management: Melanie Schöni
Copyediting: Brad Finger
Production management and typesetting:
Susanne Hermann
Printing and binding: DZS Grafik d.o.o.
Paper: Tauro

Prestel Publishing compensates the CO_2 emissions
produced from the making of this book by
supporting a reforestation project in Brazil.
Find further information on the project here:
www.ClimatePartner.com/14044-1912-1001

Penguin Random House Verlagsgruppe FSC® N001967
Printed in Slovenia
ISBN 978-3-7913-7429-1

www.prestel.com